Lancelot And Elaine

Alfred Lord Tennyson

© 2023 Culturea Editions
Texte et illustration de couverture : © domaine public
Edition : Culturea (Hérault, 34)
Contact : infos@culturea.fr
Retrouvez notre catalogue sur http://culturea.fr
Imprimé en Allemagne par Books on Demand
Design typographique : Derek Murphy
Layout : Reedsy (https://reedsy.com/)
ISBN : 9791041817443
Dépôt légal : Juin 2023

Lancelot And Elaine

Elaine the fair, Elaine the loveable,
Elaine, the lily maid of Astolat,
High in her chamber up a tower to the east
Guarded the sacred shield of Lancelot;
Which first she placed where the morning's earliest ray
Might strike it, and awake her with the gleam;
Then fearing rust or soilure fashioned for it
A case of silk, and braided thereupon
All the devices blazoned on the shield
In their own tinct, and added, of her wit,
A border fantasy of branch and flower,
And yellow-throated nestling in the nest.
Nor rested thus content, but day by day,
Leaving her household and good father, climbed
That eastern tower, and entering barred her door,
Stript off the case, and read the naked shield,
Now guessed a hidden meaning in his arms,
Now made a pretty history to herself
Of every dint a sword had beaten in it,
And every scratch a lance had made upon it,
Conjecturing when and where: this cut is fresh;
That ten years back; this dealt him at Caerlyle;
That at Caerleon; this at Camelot:
And ah God's mercy, what a stroke was there!
And here a thrust that might have killed, but God
Broke the strong lance, and rolled his enemy down,
And saved him: so she lived in fantasy.

How came the lily maid by that good shield
Of Lancelot, she that knew not even his name?
He left it with her, when he rode to tilt
For the great diamond in the diamond jousts,
Which Arthur had ordained, and by that name
Had named them, since a diamond was the prize.

For Arthur, long before they crowned him King,
Roving the trackless realms of Lyonnesse,
Had found a glen, gray boulder and black tarn.

A horror lived about the tarn, and clave
Like its own mists to all the mountain side:
For here two brothers, one a king, had met
And fought together; but their names were lost;
And each had slain his brother at a blow;
And down they fell and made the glen abhorred:
And there they lay till all their bones were bleached,
And lichened into colour with the crags:
And he, that once was king, had on a crown
Of diamonds, one in front, and four aside.
And Arthur came, and labouring up the pass,
All in a misty moonshine, unawares
Had trodden that crowned skeleton, and the skull
Brake from the nape, and from the skull the crown
Rolled into light, and turning on its rims
Fled like a glittering rivulet to the tarn:
And down the shingly scaur he plunged, and caught,
And set it on his head, and in his heart
Heard murmurs, 'Lo, thou likewise shalt be King.'

Thereafter, when a King, he had the gems
Plucked from the crown, and showed them to his knights,
Saying, 'These jewels, whereupon I chanced
Divinely, are the kingdom's, not the King's--
For public use: henceforward let there be,
Once every year, a joust for one of these:
For so by nine years' proof we needs must learn
Which is our mightiest, and ourselves shall grow
In use of arms and manhood, till we drive
The heathen, who, some say, shall rule the land
Hereafter, which God hinder.' Thus he spoke:
And eight years past, eight jousts had been, and still
Had Lancelot won the diamond of the year,
With purpose to present them to the Queen,
When all were won; but meaning all at once
To snare her royal fancy with a boon
Worth half her realm, had never spoken word.

Now for the central diamond and the last
And largest, Arthur, holding then his court

Hard on the river nigh the place which now
Is this world's hugest, let proclaim a joust
At Camelot, and when the time drew nigh
Spake (for she had been sick) to Guinevere,
'Are you so sick, my Queen, you cannot move
To these fair jousts?' 'Yea, lord,' she said, 'ye know
it.'
'Then will ye miss,' he answered, 'the great deeds
Of Lancelot, and his prowess in the lists,
A sight ye love to look on.' And the Queen
Lifted her eyes, and they dwelt languidly
On Lancelot, where he stood beside the King.
He thinking that he read her meaning there,
'Stay with me, I am sick; my love is more
Than many diamonds,' yielded; and a heart
Love-loyal to the least wish of the Queen
(However much he yearned to make complete
The tale of diamonds for his destined boon)
Urged him to speak against the truth, and say,
'Sir King, mine ancient wound is hardly whole,
And lets me from the saddle;' and the King
Glanced first at him, then her, and went his way.
No sooner gone than suddenly she began:

'To blame, my lord Sir Lancelot, much to blame!
Why go ye not to these fair jousts? the knights
Are half of them our enemies, and the crowd
Will murmur, "Lo the shameless ones, who take
Their pastime now the trustful King is gone!"'
Then Lancelot vext at having lied in vain:
'Are ye so wise? ye were not once so wise,
My Queen, that summer, when ye loved me first.
Then of the crowd ye took no more account
Than of the myriad cricket of the mead,
When its own voice clings to each blade of grass,
And every voice is nothing. As to knights,
Them surely can I silence with all ease.
But now my loyal worship is allowed
Of all men: many a bard, without offence,
Has linked our names together in his lay,

Lancelot, the flower of bravery, Guinevere,
The pearl of beauty: and our knights at feast
Have pledged us in this union, while the King
Would listen smiling. How then? is there more?
Has Arthur spoken aught? or would yourself,
Now weary of my service and devoir,
Henceforth be truer to your faultless lord?'

She broke into a little scornful laugh:
'Arthur, my lord, Arthur, the faultless King,
That passionate perfection, my good lord--
But who can gaze upon the Sun in heaven?
He never spake word of reproach to me,
He never had a glimpse of mine untruth,
He cares not for me: only here today
There gleamed a vague suspicion in his eyes:
Some meddling rogue has tampered with him--else
Rapt in this fancy of his Table Round,
And swearing men to vows impossible,
To make them like himself: but, friend, to me
He is all fault who hath no fault at all:
For who loves me must have a touch of earth;
The low sun makes the colour: I am yours,
Not Arthur's, as ye know, save by the bond.
And therefore hear my words: go to the jousts:
The tiny-trumpeting gnat can break our dream
When sweetest; and the vermin voices here
May buzz so loud--we scorn them, but they sting.'

Then answered Lancelot, the chief of knights:
'And with what face, after my pretext made,
Shall I appear, O Queen, at Camelot, I
Before a King who honours his own word,
As if it were his God's?'

'Yea,' said the Queen,
'A moral child without the craft to rule,
Else had he not lost me: but listen to me,
If I must find you wit: we hear it said
That men go down before your spear at a touch,

But knowing you are Lancelot; your great name,
This conquers: hide it therefore; go unknown:
Win! by this kiss you will: and our true King
Will then allow your pretext, O my knight,
As all for glory; for to speak him true,
Ye know right well, how meek soe'er he seem,
No keener hunter after glory breathes.
He loves it in his knights more than himself:
They prove to him his work: win and return.'

Then got Sir Lancelot suddenly to horse,
Wroth at himself. Not willing to be known,
He left the barren-beaten thoroughfare,
Chose the green path that showed the rarer foot,
And there among the solitary downs,
Full often lost in fancy, lost his way;
Till as he traced a faintly-shadowed track,
That all in loops and links among the dales
Ran to the Castle of Astolat, he saw
Fired from the west, far on a hill, the towers.
Thither he made, and blew the gateway horn.
Then came an old, dumb, myriad-wrinkled man,
Who let him into lodging and disarmed.
And Lancelot marvelled at the wordless man;
And issuing found the Lord of Astolat
With two strong sons, Sir Torre and Sir Lavaine,
Moving to meet him in the castle court;
And close behind them stept the lily maid
Elaine, his daughter: mother of the house
There was not: some light jest among them rose
With laughter dying down as the great knight
Approached them: then the Lord of Astolat:
'Whence comes thou, my guest, and by what name
Livest thou between the lips? for by thy state
And presence I might guess thee chief of those,
After the King, who eat in Arthur's halls.
Him have I seen: the rest, his Table Round,
Known as they are, to me they are unknown.'

Then answered Sir Lancelot, the chief of knights:

'Known am I, and of Arthur's hall, and known,
What I by mere mischance have brought, my shield.
But since I go to joust as one unknown
At Camelot for the diamond, ask me not,
Hereafter ye shall know me--and the shield--
I pray you lend me one, if such you have,
Blank, or at least with some device not mine.'

Then said the Lord of Astolat, 'Here is Torre's:
Hurt in his first tilt was my son, Sir Torre.
And so, God wot, his shield is blank enough.
His ye can have.' Then added plain Sir Torre,
'Yea, since I cannot use it, ye may have it.'
Here laughed the father saying, 'Fie, Sir Churl,
Is that answer for a noble knight?
Allow him! but Lavaine, my younger here,
He is so full of lustihood, he will ride,
Joust for it, and win, and bring it in an hour,
And set it in this damsel's golden hair,
To make her thrice as wilful as before.'

'Nay, father, nay good father, shame me not
Before this noble knight,' said young Lavaine,
'For nothing. Surely I but played on Torre:
He seemed so sullen, vext he could not go:
A jest, no more! for, knight, the maiden dreamt
That some one put this diamond in her hand,
And that it was too slippery to be held,
And slipt and fell into some pool or stream,
The castle-well, belike; and then I said
That IF I went and IF I fought and won it
(But all was jest and joke among ourselves)
Then must she keep it safelier. All was jest.
But, father, give me leave, an if he will,
To ride to Camelot with this noble knight:
Win shall I not, but do my best to win:
Young as I am, yet would I do my best.'

'So will ye grace me,' answered Lancelot,
Smiling a moment, 'with your fellowship

O'er these waste downs whereon I lost myself,
Then were I glad of you as guide and friend:
And you shall win this diamond,--as I hear
It is a fair large diamond,--if ye may,
And yield it to this maiden, if ye will.'
'A fair large diamond,' added plain Sir Torre,
'Such be for queens, and not for simple maids.'
Then she, who held her eyes upon the ground,
Elaine, and heard her name so tost about,
Flushed slightly at the slight disparagement
Before the stranger knight, who, looking at her,
Full courtly, yet not falsely, thus returned:
'If what is fair be but for what is fair,
And only queens are to be counted so,
Rash were my judgment then, who deem this maid
Might wear as fair a jewel as is on earth,
Not violating the bond of like to like.'

He spoke and ceased: the lily maid Elaine,
Won by the mellow voice before she looked,
Lifted her eyes, and read his lineaments.
The great and guilty love he bare the Queen,
In battle with the love he bare his lord,
Had marred his face, and marked it ere his time.
Another sinning on such heights with one,
The flower of all the west and all the world,
Had been the sleeker for it: but in him
His mood was often like a fiend, and rose
And drove him into wastes and solitudes
For agony, who was yet a living soul.
Marred as he was, he seemed the goodliest man
That ever among ladies ate in hall,
And noblest, when she lifted up her eyes.
However marred, of more than twice her years,
Seamed with an ancient swordcut on the cheek,
And bruised and bronzed, she lifted up her eyes
And loved him, with that love which was her doom.

Then the great knight, the darling of the court,
Loved of the loveliest, into that rude hall

Stept with all grace, and not with half disdain
Hid under grace, as in a smaller time,
But kindly man moving among his kind:
Whom they with meats and vintage of their best
And talk and minstrel melody entertained.
And much they asked of court and Table Round,
And ever well and readily answered he:
But Lancelot, when they glanced at Guinevere,
Suddenly speaking of the wordless man,
Heard from the Baron that, ten years before,
The heathen caught and reft him of his tongue.
'He learnt and warned me of their fierce design
Against my house, and him they caught and maimed;
But I, my sons, and little daughter fled
From bonds or death, and dwelt among the woods
By the great river in a boatman's hut.
Dull days were those, till our good Arthur broke
The Pagan yet once more on Badon hill.'

'O there, great lord, doubtless,' Lavaine said, rapt
By all the sweet and sudden passion of youth
Toward greatness in its elder, 'you have fought.
O tell us--for we live apart--you know
Of Arthur's glorious wars.' And Lancelot spoke
And answered him at full, as having been
With Arthur in the fight which all day long
Rang by the white mouth of the violent Glem;
And in the four loud battles by the shore
Of Duglas; that on Bassa; then the war
That thundered in and out the gloomy skirts
Of Celidon the forest; and again
By castle Gurnion, where the glorious King
Had on his cuirass worn our Lady's Head,
Carved of one emerald centered in a sun
Of silver rays, that lightened as he breathed;
And at Caerleon had he helped his lord,
When the strong neighings of the wild white Horse
Set every gilded parapet shuddering;
And up in Agned-Cathregonion too,
And down the waste sand-shores of Trath Treroit,

Where many a heathen fell; 'and on the mount
Of Badon I myself beheld the King
Charge at the head of all his Table Round,
And all his legions crying Christ and him,
And break them; and I saw him, after, stand
High on a heap of slain, from spur to plume
Red as the rising sun with heathen blood,
And seeing me, with a great voice he cried,
"They are broken, they are broken!" for the King,
However mild he seems at home, nor cares
For triumph in our mimic wars, the jousts--
For if his own knight cast him down, he laughs
Saying, his knights are better men than he--
Yet in this heathen war the fire of God
Fills him: I never saw his like: there lives
No greater leader.'

While he uttered this,
Low to her own heart said the lily maid,
'Save your own great self, fair lord;' and when he fell
From talk of war to traits of pleasantry--
Being mirthful he, but in a stately kind--
She still took note that when the living smile
Died from his lips, across him came a cloud
Of melancholy severe, from which again,
Whenever in her hovering to and fro
The lily maid had striven to make him cheer,
There brake a sudden-beaming tenderness
Of manners and of nature: and she thought
That all was nature, all, perchance, for her.
And all night long his face before her lived,
As when a painter, poring on a face,
Divinely through all hindrance finds the man
Behind it, and so paints him that his face,
The shape and colour of a mind and life,
Lives for his children, ever at its best
And fullest; so the face before her lived,
Dark-splendid, speaking in the silence, full
Of noble things, and held her from her sleep.
Till rathe she rose, half-cheated in the thought

She needs must bid farewell to sweet Lavaine.
First in fear, step after step, she stole
Down the long tower-stairs, hesitating:
Anon, she heard Sir Lancelot cry in the court,
'This shield, my friend, where is it?' and Lavaine
Past inward, as she came from out the tower.
There to his proud horse Lancelot turned, and smoothed
The glossy shoulder, humming to himself.
Half-envious of the flattering hand, she drew
Nearer and stood. He looked, and more amazed
Than if seven men had set upon him, saw
The maiden standing in the dewy light.
He had not dreamed she was so beautiful.
Then came on him a sort of sacred fear,
For silent, though he greeted her, she stood
Rapt on his face as if it were a God's.
Suddenly flashed on her a wild desire,
That he should wear her favour at the tilt.
She braved a riotous heart in asking for it.
'Fair lord, whose name I know not--noble it is,
I well believe, the noblest--will you wear
My favour at this tourney?' 'Nay,' said he,
'Fair lady, since I never yet have worn
Favour of any lady in the lists.
Such is my wont, as those, who know me, know.'
'Yea, so,' she answered; 'then in wearing mine
Needs must be lesser likelihood, noble lord,
That those who know should know you.' And he turned
Her counsel up and down within his mind,
And found it true, and answered, 'True, my child.
Well, I will wear it: fetch it out to me:
What is it?' and she told him 'A red sleeve
Broidered with pearls,' and brought it: then he bound
Her token on his helmet, with a smile
Saying, 'I never yet have done so much
For any maiden living,' and the blood
Sprang to her face and filled her with delight;
But left her all the paler, when Lavaine
Returning brought the yet-unblazoned shield,
His brother's; which he gave to Lancelot,

Who parted with his own to fair Elaine:
'Do me this grace, my child, to have my shield
In keeping till I come.' 'A grace to me,'
She answered, 'twice today. I am your squire!'
Whereat Lavaine said, laughing, 'Lily maid,
For fear our people call you lily maid
In earnest, let me bring your colour back;
Once, twice, and thrice: now get you hence to bed:'
So kissed her, and Sir Lancelot his own hand,
And thus they moved away: she stayed a minute,
Then made a sudden step to the gate, and there--
Her bright hair blown about the serious face
Yet rosy-kindled with her brother's kiss--
Paused by the gateway, standing near the shield
In silence, while she watched their arms far-off
Sparkle, until they dipt below the downs.
Then to her tower she climbed, and took the shield,
There kept it, and so lived in fantasy.

Meanwhile the new companions past away
Far o'er the long backs of the bushless downs,
To where Sir Lancelot knew there lived a knight
Not far from Camelot, now for forty years
A hermit, who had prayed, laboured and prayed,
And ever labouring had scooped himself
In the white rock a chapel and a hall
On massive columns, like a shorecliff cave,
And cells and chambers: all were fair and dry;
The green light from the meadows underneath
Struck up and lived along the milky roofs;
And in the meadows tremulous aspen-trees
And poplars made a noise of falling showers.
And thither wending there that night they bode.

But when the next day broke from underground,
And shot red fire and shadows through the cave,
They rose, heard mass, broke fast, and rode away:
Then Lancelot saying, 'Hear, but hold my name
Hidden, you ride with Lancelot of the Lake,'
Abashed young Lavaine, whose instant reverence,

Dearer to true young hearts than their own praise,
But left him leave to stammer, 'Is it indeed?'
And after muttering 'The great Lancelot,
At last he got his breath and answered, 'One,
One have I seen--that other, our liege lord,
The dread Pendragon, Britain's King of kings,
Of whom the people talk mysteriously,
He will be there--then were I stricken blind
That minute, I might say that I had seen.'

So spake Lavaine, and when they reached the lists
By Camelot in the meadow, let his eyes
Run through the peopled gallery which half round
Lay like a rainbow fallen upon the grass,
Until they found the clear-faced King, who sat
Robed in red samite, easily to be known,
Since to his crown the golden dragon clung,
And down his robe the dragon writhed in gold,
And from the carven-work behind him crept
Two dragons gilded, sloping down to make
Arms for his chair, while all the rest of them
Through knots and loops and folds innumerable
Fled ever through the woodwork, till they found
The new design wherein they lost themselves,
Yet with all ease, so tender was the work:
And, in the costly canopy o'er him set,
Blazed the last diamond of the nameless king.

Then Lancelot answered young Lavaine and said,
'Me you call great: mine is the firmer seat,
The truer lance: but there is many a youth
Now crescent, who will come to all I am
And overcome it; and in me there dwells
No greatness, save it be some far-off touch
Of greatness to know well I am not great:
There is the man.' And Lavaine gaped upon him
As on a thing miraculous, and anon
The trumpets blew; and then did either side,
They that assailed, and they that held the lists,
Set lance in rest, strike spur, suddenly move,

Meet in the midst, and there so furiously
Shock, that a man far-off might well perceive,
If any man that day were left afield,
The hard earth shake, and a low thunder of arms.
And Lancelot bode a little, till he saw
Which were the weaker; then he hurled into it
Against the stronger: little need to speak
Of Lancelot in his glory! King, duke, earl,
Count, baron--whom he smote, he overthrew.

But in the field were Lancelot's kith and kin,
Ranged with the Table Round that held the lists,
Strong men, and wrathful that a stranger knight
Should do and almost overdo the deeds
Of Lancelot; and one said to the other, 'Lo!
What is he? I do not mean the force alone--
The grace and versatility of the man!
Is it not Lancelot?' 'When has Lancelot worn
Favour of any lady in the lists?
Not such his wont, as we, that know him, know.'
'How then? who then?' a fury seized them all,
A fiery family passion for the name
Of Lancelot, and a glory one with theirs.
They couched their spears and pricked their steeds, and
thus,
Their plumes driven backward by the wind they made
In moving, all together down upon him
Bare, as a wild wave in the wide North-sea,
Green-glimmering toward the summit, bears, with all
Its stormy crests that smoke against the skies,
Down on a bark, and overbears the bark,
And him that helms it, so they overbore
Sir Lancelot and his charger, and a spear
Down-glancing lamed the charger, and a spear
Pricked sharply his own cuirass, and the head
Pierced through his side, and there snapt, and
remained.

Then Sir Lavaine did well and worshipfully;
He bore a knight of old repute to the earth,

And brought his horse to Lancelot where he lay.
He up the side, sweating with agony, got,
But thought to do while he might yet endure,
And being lustily holpen by the rest,
His party,--though it seemed half-miracle
To those he fought with,--drave his kith and kin,
And all the Table Round that held the lists,
Back to the barrier; then the trumpets blew
Proclaiming his the prize, who wore the sleeve
Of scarlet, and the pearls; and all the knights,
His party, cried 'Advance and take thy prize
The diamond;' but he answered, 'Diamond me
No diamonds! for God's love, a little air!
Prize me no prizes, for my prize is death!
Hence will I, and I charge you, follow me not.'

He spoke, and vanished suddenly from the field
With young Lavaine into the poplar grove.
There from his charger down he slid, and sat,
Gasping to Sir Lavaine, 'Draw the lance-head:'
'Ah my sweet lord Sir Lancelot,' said Lavaine,
'I dread me, if I draw it, you will die.'
But he, 'I die already with it: draw--
Draw,'--and Lavaine drew, and Sir Lancelot gave
A marvellous great shriek and ghastly groan,
And half his blood burst forth, and down he sank
For the pure pain, and wholly swooned away.
Then came the hermit out and bare him in,
There stanched his wound; and there, in daily doubt
Whether to live or die, for many a week
Hid from the wide world's rumour by the grove
Of poplars with their noise of falling showers,
And ever-tremulous aspen-trees, he lay.

But on that day when Lancelot fled the lists,
His party, knights of utmost North and West,
Lords of waste marches, kings of desolate isles,
Came round their great Pendragon, saying to him,
'Lo, Sire, our knight, through whom we won the day,
Hath gone sore wounded, and hath left his prize

Untaken, crying that his prize is death.'
'Heaven hinder,' said the King, 'that such an one,
So great a knight as we have seen today--
He seemed to me another Lancelot--
Yea, twenty times I thought him Lancelot--
He must not pass uncared for. Wherefore, rise,
O Gawain, and ride forth and find the knight.
Wounded and wearied needs must he be near.
I charge you that you get at once to horse.
And, knights and kings, there breathes not one of you
Will deem this prize of ours is rashly given:
His prowess was too wondrous. We will do him
No customary honour: since the knight
Came not to us, of us to claim the prize,
Ourselves will send it after. Rise and take
This diamond, and deliver it, and return,
And bring us where he is, and how he fares,
And cease not from your quest until ye find.'

So saying, from the carven flower above,
To which it made a restless heart, he took,
And gave, the diamond: then from where he sat
At Arthur's right, with smiling face arose,
With smiling face and frowning heart, a Prince
In the mid might and flourish of his May,
Gawain, surnamed The Courteous, fair and strong,
And after Lancelot, Tristram, and Geraint
And Gareth, a good knight, but therewithal
Sir Modred's brother, and the child of Lot,
Nor often loyal to his word, and now
Wroth that the King's command to sally forth
In quest of whom he knew not, made him leave
The banquet, and concourse of knights and kings.

So all in wrath he got to horse and went;
While Arthur to the banquet, dark in mood,
Past, thinking 'Is it Lancelot who hath come
Despite the wound he spake of, all for gain
Of glory, and hath added wound to wound,
And ridden away to die?' So feared the King,

And, after two days' tarriance there, returned.
Then when he saw the Queen, embracing asked,
'Love, are you yet so sick?' 'Nay, lord,' she said.
'And where is Lancelot?' Then the Queen amazed,
'Was he not with you? won he not your prize?'
'Nay, but one like him.' 'Why that like was he.'
And when the King demanded how she knew,
Said, 'Lord, no sooner had ye parted from us,
Than Lancelot told me of a common talk
That men went down before his spear at a touch,
But knowing he was Lancelot; his great name
Conquered; and therefore would he hide his name
From all men, even the King, and to this end
Had made a pretext of a hindering wound,
That he might joust unknown of all, and learn
If his old prowess were in aught decayed;
And added, "Our true Arthur, when he learns,
Will well allow me pretext, as for gain
Of purer glory."'

Then replied the King:
'Far lovelier in our Lancelot had it been,
In lieu of idly dallying with the truth,
To have trusted me as he hath trusted thee.
Surely his King and most familiar friend
Might well have kept his secret. True, indeed,
Albeit I know my knights fantastical,
So fine a fear in our large Lancelot
Must needs have moved my laughter: now remains
But little cause for laughter: his own kin--
Ill news, my Queen, for all who love him, this!--
His kith and kin, not knowing, set upon him;
So that he went sore wounded from the field:
Yet good news too: for goodly hopes are mine
That Lancelot is no more a lonely heart.
He wore, against his wont, upon his helm
A sleeve of scarlet, broidered with great pearls,
Some gentle maiden's gift.'

'Yea, lord,' she said,

'Thy hopes are mine,' and saying that, she choked,
And sharply turned about to hide her face,
Past to her chamber, and there flung herself
Down on the great King's couch, and writhed upon it,
And clenched her fingers till they bit the palm,
And shrieked out 'Traitor' to the unhearing wall,
Then flashed into wild tears, and rose again,
And moved about her palace, proud and pale.

Gawain the while through all the region round
Rode with his diamond, wearied of the quest,
Touched at all points, except the poplar grove,
And came at last, though late, to Astolat:
Whom glittering in enamelled arms the maid
Glanced at, and cried, 'What news from Camelot, lord?
What of the knight with the red sleeve?' 'He won.'
'I knew it,' she said. 'But parted from the jousts
Hurt in the side,' whereat she caught her breath;
Through her own side she felt the sharp lance go;
Thereon she smote her hand: wellnigh she swooned:
And, while he gazed wonderingly at her, came
The Lord of Astolat out, to whom the Prince
Reported who he was, and on what quest
Sent, that he bore the prize and could not find
The victor, but had ridden a random round
To seek him, and had wearied of the search.
To whom the Lord of Astolat, 'Bide with us,
And ride no more at random, noble Prince!
Here was the knight, and here he left a shield;
This will he send or come for: furthermore
Our son is with him; we shall hear anon,
Needs must hear.' To this the courteous Prince
Accorded with his wonted courtesy,
Courtesy with a touch of traitor in it,
And stayed; and cast his eyes on fair Elaine:
Where could be found face daintier? then her shape
From forehead down to foot, perfect--again
From foot to forehead exquisitely turned:
'Well--if I bide, lo! this wild flower for me!'
And oft they met among the garden yews,

And there he set himself to play upon her
With sallying wit, free flashes from a height
Above her, graces of the court, and songs,
Sighs, and slow smiles, and golden eloquence
And amorous adulation, till the maid
Rebelled against it, saying to him, 'Prince,
O loyal nephew of our noble King,
Why ask you not to see the shield he left,
Whence you might learn his name? Why slight your King,
And lose the quest he sent you on, and prove
No surer than our falcon yesterday,
Who lost the hern we slipt her at, and went
To all the winds?' 'Nay, by mine head,' said he,
'I lose it, as we lose the lark in heaven,
O damsel, in the light of your blue eyes;
But an ye will it let me see the shield.'
And when the shield was brought, and Gawain saw
Sir Lancelot's azure lions, crowned with gold,
Ramp in the field, he smote his thigh, and mocked:
'Right was the King! our Lancelot! that true man!'
'And right was I,' she answered merrily, 'I,
Who dreamed my knight the greatest knight of all.'
'And if I dreamed,' said Gawain, 'that you love
This greatest knight, your pardon! lo, ye know it!
Speak therefore: shall I waste myself in vain?'
Full simple was her answer, 'What know I?
My brethren have been all my fellowship;
And I, when often they have talked of love,
Wished it had been my mother, for they talked,
Meseemed, of what they knew not; so myself--
I know not if I know what true love is,
But if I know, then, if I love not him,
I know there is none other I can love.'
'Yea, by God's death,' said he, 'ye love him well,
But would not, knew ye what all others know,
And whom he loves.' 'So be it,' cried Elaine,
And lifted her fair face and moved away:
But he pursued her, calling, 'Stay a little!
One golden minute's grace! he wore your sleeve:
Would he break faith with one I may not name?

Must our true man change like a leaf at last?
Nay--like enow: why then, far be it from me
To cross our mighty Lancelot in his loves!
And, damsel, for I deem you know full well
Where your great knight is hidden, let me leave
My quest with you; the diamond also: here!
For if you love, it will be sweet to give it;
And if he love, it will be sweet to have it
From your own hand; and whether he love or not,
A diamond is a diamond. Fare you well
A thousand times!--a thousand times farewell!
Yet, if he love, and his love hold, we two
May meet at court hereafter: there, I think,
So ye will learn the courtesies of the court,
We two shall know each other.'

Then he gave,
And slightly kissed the hand to which he gave,
The diamond, and all wearied of the quest
Leapt on his horse, and carolling as he went
A true-love ballad, lightly rode away.

Thence to the court he past; there told the King
What the King knew, 'Sir Lancelot is the knight.'
And added, 'Sire, my liege, so much I learnt;
But failed to find him, though I rode all round
The region: but I lighted on the maid
Whose sleeve he wore; she loves him; and to her,
Deeming our courtesy is the truest law,
I gave the diamond: she will render it;
For by mine head she knows his hiding-place.'

The seldom-frowning King frowned, and replied,
'Too courteous truly! ye shall go no more
On quest of mine, seeing that ye forget
Obedience is the courtesy due to kings.'

He spake and parted. Wroth, but all in awe,
For twenty strokes of the blood, without a word,
Lingered that other, staring after him;

Then shook his hair, strode off, and buzzed abroad
About the maid of Astolat, and her love.
All ears were pricked at once, all tongues were loosed:
'The maid of Astolat loves Sir Lancelot,
Sir Lancelot loves the maid of Astolat.'
Some read the King's face, some the Queen's, and all
Had marvel what the maid might be, but most
Predoomed her as unworthy. One old dame
Came suddenly on the Queen with the sharp news.
She, that had heard the noise of it before,
But sorrowing Lancelot should have stooped so low,
Marred her friend's aim with pale tranquillity.
So ran the tale like fire about the court,
Fire in dry stubble a nine-days' wonder flared:
Till even the knights at banquet twice or thrice
Forgot to drink to Lancelot and the Queen,
And pledging Lancelot and the lily maid
Smiled at each other, while the Queen, who sat
With lips severely placid, felt the knot
Climb in her throat, and with her feet unseen
Crushed the wild passion out against the floor
Beneath the banquet, where all the meats became
As wormwood, and she hated all who pledged.

But far away the maid in Astolat,
Her guiltless rival, she that ever kept
The one-day-seen Sir Lancelot in her heart,
Crept to her father, while he mused alone,
Sat on his knee, stroked his gray face and said,
'Father, you call me wilful, and the fault
Is yours who let me have my will, and now,
Sweet father, will you let me lose my wits?'
'Nay,' said he, 'surely.' 'Wherefore, let me hence,'
She answered, 'and find out our dear Lavaine.'
'Ye will not lose your wits for dear Lavaine:
Bide,' answered he: 'we needs must hear anon
Of him, and of that other.' 'Ay,' she said,
'And of that other, for I needs must hence
And find that other, wheresoe'er he be,
And with mine own hand give his diamond to him,

Lest I be found as faithless in the quest
As yon proud Prince who left the quest to me.
Sweet father, I behold him in my dreams
Gaunt as it were the skeleton of himself,
Death-pale, for lack of gentle maiden's aid.
The gentler-born the maiden, the more bound,
My father, to be sweet and serviceable
To noble knights in sickness, as ye know
When these have worn their tokens: let me hence
I pray you.' Then her father nodding said,
'Ay, ay, the diamond: wit ye well, my child,
Right fain were I to learn this knight were whole,
Being our greatest: yea, and you must give it--
And sure I think this fruit is hung too high
For any mouth to gape for save a queen's--
Nay, I mean nothing: so then, get you gone,
Being so very wilful you must go.'

Lightly, her suit allowed, she slipt away,
And while she made her ready for her ride,
Her father's latest word hummed in her ear,
'Being so very wilful you must go,'
And changed itself and echoed in her heart,
'Being so very wilful you must die.'
But she was happy enough and shook it off,
As we shake off the bee that buzzes at us;
And in her heart she answered it and said,
'What matter, so I help him back to life?'
Then far away with good Sir Torre for guide
Rode o'er the long backs of the bushless downs
To Camelot, and before the city-gates
Came on her brother with a happy face
Making a roan horse caper and curvet
For pleasure all about a field of flowers:
Whom when she saw, 'Lavaine,' she cried, 'Lavaine,
How fares my lord Sir Lancelot?' He amazed,
'Torre and Elaine! why here? Sir Lancelot!
How know ye my lord's name is Lancelot?'
But when the maid had told him all her tale,
Then turned Sir Torre, and being in his moods

Left them, and under the strange-statued gate,
Where Arthur's wars were rendered mystically,
Past up the still rich city to his kin,
His own far blood, which dwelt at Camelot;
And her, Lavaine across the poplar grove
Led to the caves: there first she saw the casque
Of Lancelot on the wall: her scarlet sleeve,
Though carved and cut, and half the pearls away,
Streamed from it still; and in her heart she laughed,
Because he had not loosed it from his helm,
But meant once more perchance to tourney in it.
And when they gained the cell wherein he slept,
His battle-writhen arms and mighty hands
Lay naked on the wolfskin, and a dream
Of dragging down his enemy made them move.
Then she that saw him lying unsleek, unshorn,
Gaunt as it were the skeleton of himself,
Uttered a little tender dolorous cry.
The sound not wonted in a place so still
Woke the sick knight, and while he rolled his eyes
Yet blank from sleep, she started to him, saying,
'Your prize the diamond sent you by the King:'
His eyes glistened: she fancied 'Is it for me?'
And when the maid had told him all the tale
Of King and Prince, the diamond sent, the quest
Assigned to her not worthy of it, she knelt
Full lowly by the corners of his bed,
And laid the diamond in his open hand.
Her face was near, and as we kiss the child
That does the task assigned, he kissed her face.
At once she slipt like water to the floor.
'Alas,' he said, 'your ride hath wearied you.
Rest must you have.' 'No rest for me,' she said;
'Nay, for near you, fair lord, I am at rest.'
What might she mean by that? his large black eyes,
Yet larger through his leanness, dwelt upon her,
Till all her heart's sad secret blazed itself
In the heart's colours on her simple face;
And Lancelot looked and was perplext in mind,
And being weak in body said no more;

But did not love the colour; woman's love,
Save one, he not regarded, and so turned
Sighing, and feigned a sleep until he slept.

Then rose Elaine and glided through the fields,
And past beneath the weirdly-sculptured gates
Far up the dim rich city to her kin;
There bode the night: but woke with dawn, and past
Down through the dim rich city to the fields,
Thence to the cave: so day by day she past
In either twilight ghost-like to and fro
Gliding, and every day she tended him,
And likewise many a night: and Lancelot
Would, though he called his wound a little hurt
Whereof he should be quickly whole, at times
Brain-feverous in his heat and agony, seem
Uncourteous, even he: but the meek maid
Sweetly forbore him ever, being to him
Meeker than any child to a rough nurse,
Milder than any mother to a sick child,
And never woman yet, since man's first fall,
Did kindlier unto man, but her deep love
Upbore her; till the hermit, skilled in all
The simples and the science of that time,
Told him that her fine care had saved his life.
And the sick man forgot her simple blush,
Would call her friend and sister, sweet Elaine,
Would listen for her coming and regret
Her parting step, and held her tenderly,
And loved her with all love except the love
Of man and woman when they love their best,
Closest and sweetest, and had died the death
In any knightly fashion for her sake.
And peradventure had he seen her first
She might have made this and that other world
Another world for the sick man; but now
The shackles of an old love straitened him,
His honour rooted in dishonour stood,
And faith unfaithful kept him falsely true.

Yet the great knight in his mid-sickness made
Full many a holy vow and pure resolve.
These, as but born of sickness, could not live:
For when the blood ran lustier in him again,
Full often the bright image of one face,
Making a treacherous quiet in his heart,
Dispersed his resolution like a cloud.
Then if the maiden, while that ghostly grace
Beamed on his fancy, spoke, he answered not,
Or short and coldly, and she knew right well
What the rough sickness meant, but what this meant
She knew not, and the sorrow dimmed her sight,
And drave her ere her time across the fields
Far into the rich city, where alone
She murmured, 'Vain, in vain: it cannot be.
He will not love me: how then? must I die?'
Then as a little helpless innocent bird,
That has but one plain passage of few notes,
Will sing the simple passage o'er and o'er
For all an April morning, till the ear
Wearies to hear it, so the simple maid
Went half the night repeating, 'Must I die?'
And now to right she turned, and now to left,
And found no ease in turning or in rest;
And 'Him or death,' she muttered, 'death or him,'
Again and like a burthen, 'Him or death.'

But when Sir Lancelot's deadly hurt was whole,
To Astolat returning rode the three.
There morn by morn, arraying her sweet self
In that wherein she deemed she looked her best,
She came before Sir Lancelot, for she thought
'If I be loved, these are my festal robes,
If not, the victim's flowers before he fall.'
And Lancelot ever prest upon the maid
That she should ask some goodly gift of him
For her own self or hers; 'and do not shun
To speak the wish most near to your true heart;
Such service have ye done me, that I make
My will of yours, and Prince and Lord am I

In mine own land, and what I will I can.'
Then like a ghost she lifted up her face,
But like a ghost without the power to speak.
And Lancelot saw that she withheld her wish,
And bode among them yet a little space
Till he should learn it; and one morn it chanced
He found her in among the garden yews,
And said, 'Delay no longer, speak your wish,
Seeing I go today:' then out she brake:
'Going? and we shall never see you more.
And I must die for want of one bold word.'
'Speak: that I live to hear,' he said, 'is yours.'
Then suddenly and passionately she spoke:
'I have gone mad. I love you: let me die.'
'Ah, sister,' answered Lancelot, 'what is this?'
And innocently extending her white arms,
'Your love,' she said, 'your love--to be your wife.'
And Lancelot answered, 'Had I chosen to wed,
I had been wedded earlier, sweet Elaine:
But now there never will be wife of mine.'
'No, no,' she cried, 'I care not to be wife,
But to be with you still, to see your face,
To serve you, and to follow you through the world.'
And Lancelot answered, 'Nay, the world, the world,
All ear and eye, with such a stupid heart
To interpret ear and eye, and such a tongue
To blare its own interpretation--nay,
Full ill then should I quit your brother's love,
And your good father's kindness.' And she said,
'Not to be with you, not to see your face--
Alas for me then, my good days are done.'
'Nay, noble maid,' he answered, 'ten times nay!
This is not love: but love's first flash in youth,
Most common: yea, I know it of mine own self:
And you yourself will smile at your own self
Hereafter, when you yield your flower of life
To one more fitly yours, not thrice your age:
And then will I, for true you are and sweet
Beyond mine old belief in womanhood,
More specially should your good knight be poor,

Endow you with broad land and territory
Even to the half my realm beyond the seas,
So that would make you happy: furthermore,
Even to the death, as though ye were my blood,
In all your quarrels will I be your knight.
This I will do, dear damsel, for your sake,
And more than this I cannot.'

While he spoke
She neither blushed nor shook, but deathly-pale
Stood grasping what was nearest, then replied:
'Of all this will I nothing;' and so fell,
And thus they bore her swooning to her tower.

Then spake, to whom through those black walls of yew
Their talk had pierced, her father: 'Ay, a flash,
I fear me, that will strike my blossom dead.
Too courteous are ye, fair Lord Lancelot.
I pray you, use some rough discourtesy
To blunt or break her passion.'
Lancelot said,
'That were against me: what I can I will;'
And there that day remained, and toward even
Sent for his shield: full meekly rose the maid,
Stript off the case, and gave the naked shield;
Then, when she heard his horse upon the stones,
Unclasping flung the casement back, and looked
Down on his helm, from which her sleeve had gone.
And Lancelot knew the little clinking sound;
And she by tact of love was well aware
That Lancelot knew that she was looking at him.
And yet he glanced not up, nor waved his hand,
Nor bad farewell, but sadly rode away.
This was the one discourtesy that he used.

So in her tower alone the maiden sat:
His very shield was gone; only the case,
Her own poor work, her empty labour, left.
But still she heard him, still his picture formed
And grew between her and the pictured wall.

Then came her father, saying in low tones,
'Have comfort,' whom she greeted quietly.
Then came her brethren saying, 'Peace to thee,
Sweet sister,' whom she answered with all calm.
But when they left her to herself again,
Death, like a friend's voice from a distant field
Approaching through the darkness, called; the owls
Wailing had power upon her, and she mixt
Her fancies with the sallow-rifted glooms
Of evening, and the moanings of the wind.

And in those days she made a little song,
And called her song 'The Song of Love and Death,'
And sang it: sweetly could she make and sing.

'Sweet is true love though given in vain, in vain;
And sweet is death who puts an end to pain:
I know not which is sweeter, no, not I.

'Love, art thou sweet? then bitter death must be:
Love, thou art bitter; sweet is death to me.
O Love, if death be sweeter, let me die.

'Sweet love, that seems not made to fade away,
Sweet death, that seems to make us loveless clay,
I know not which is sweeter, no, not I.

'I fain would follow love, if that could be;
I needs must follow death, who calls for me;
Call and I follow, I follow! let me die.'

High with the last line scaled her voice, and this,
All in a fiery dawning wild with wind
That shook her tower, the brothers heard, and thought
With shuddering, 'Hark the Phantom of the house
That ever shrieks before a death,' and called
The father, and all three in hurry and fear
Ran to her, and lo! the blood-red light of dawn
Flared on her face, she shrilling, 'Let me die!'

As when we dwell upon a word we know,
Repeating, till the word we know so well
Becomes a wonder, and we know not why,
So dwelt the father on her face, and thought
'Is this Elaine?' till back the maiden fell,
Then gave a languid hand to each, and lay,
Speaking a still good-morrow with her eyes.
At last she said, 'Sweet brothers, yesternight
I seemed a curious little maid again,
As happy as when we dwelt among the woods,
And when ye used to take me with the flood
Up the great river in the boatman's boat.
Only ye would not pass beyond the cape
That has the poplar on it: there ye fixt
Your limit, oft returning with the tide.
And yet I cried because ye would not pass
Beyond it, and far up the shining flood
Until we found the palace of the King.
And yet ye would not; but this night I dreamed
That I was all alone upon the flood,
And then I said, "Now shall I have my will:"
And there I woke, but still the wish remained.
So let me hence that I may pass at last
Beyond the poplar and far up the flood,
Until I find the palace of the King.
There will I enter in among them all,
And no man there will dare to mock at me;
But there the fine Gawain will wonder at me,
And there the great Sir Lancelot muse at me;
Gawain, who bad a thousand farewells to me,
Lancelot, who coldly went, nor bad me one:
And there the King will know me and my love,
And there the Queen herself will pity me,
And all the gentle court will welcome me,
And after my long voyage I shall rest!'

'Peace,' said her father, 'O my child, ye seem
Light-headed, for what force is yours to go
So far, being sick? and wherefore would ye look
On this proud fellow again, who scorns us all?'

Then the rough Torre began to heave and move,
And bluster into stormy sobs and say,
'I never loved him: an I meet with him,
I care not howsoever great he be,
Then will I strike at him and strike him down,
Give me good fortune, I will strike him dead,
For this discomfort he hath done the house.'

To whom the gentle sister made reply,
'Fret not yourself, dear brother, nor be wroth,
Seeing it is no more Sir Lancelot's fault
Not to love me, than it is mine to love
Him of all men who seems to me the highest.'

'Highest?' the father answered, echoing 'highest?'
(He meant to break the passion in her) 'nay,
Daughter, I know not what you call the highest;
But this I know, for all the people know it,
He loves the Queen, and in an open shame:
And she returns his love in open shame;
If this be high, what is it to be low?'

Then spake the lily maid of Astolat:
'Sweet father, all too faint and sick am I
For anger: these are slanders: never yet
Was noble man but made ignoble talk.
He makes no friend who never made a foe.
But now it is my glory to have loved
One peerless, without stain: so let me pass,
My father, howsoe'er I seem to you,
Not all unhappy, having loved God's best
And greatest, though my love had no return:
Yet, seeing you desire your child to live,
Thanks, but you work against your own desire;
For if I could believe the things you say
I should but die the sooner; wherefore cease,
Sweet father, and bid call the ghostly man
Hither, and let me shrive me clean, and die.'

So when the ghostly man had come and gone,
She with a face, bright as for sin forgiven,
Besought Lavaine to write as she devised
A letter, word for word; and when he asked
'Is it for Lancelot, is it for my dear lord?
Then will I bear it gladly;' she replied,
'For Lancelot and the Queen and all the world,
But I myself must bear it.' Then he wrote
The letter she devised; which being writ
And folded, 'O sweet father, tender and true,
Deny me not,' she said--'ye never yet
Denied my fancies--this, however strange,
My latest: lay the letter in my hand
A little ere I die, and close the hand
Upon it; I shall guard it even in death.
And when the heat is gone from out my heart,
Then take the little bed on which I died
For Lancelot's love, and deck it like the Queen's
For richness, and me also like the Queen
In all I have of rich, and lay me on it.
And let there be prepared a chariot-bier
To take me to the river, and a barge
Be ready on the river, clothed in black.
I go in state to court, to meet the Queen.
There surely I shall speak for mine own self,
And none of you can speak for me so well.
And therefore let our dumb old man alone
Go with me, he can steer and row, and he
Will guide me to that palace, to the doors.'

She ceased: her father promised; whereupon
She grew so cheerful that they deemed her death
Was rather in the fantasy than the blood.
But ten slow mornings past, and on the eleventh
Her father laid the letter in her hand,
And closed the hand upon it, and she died.
So that day there was dole in Astolat.

But when the next sun brake from underground,
Then, those two brethren slowly with bent brows

Accompanying, the sad chariot-bier
Past like a shadow through the field, that shone
Full-summer, to that stream whereon the barge,
Palled all its length in blackest samite, lay.
There sat the lifelong creature of the house,
Loyal, the dumb old servitor, on deck,
Winking his eyes, and twisted all his face.
So those two brethren from the chariot took
And on the black decks laid her in her bed,
Set in her hand a lily, o'er her hung
The silken case with braided blazonings,
And kissed her quiet brows, and saying to her
'Sister, farewell for ever,' and again
'Farewell, sweet sister,' parted all in tears.
Then rose the dumb old servitor, and the dead,
Oared by the dumb, went upward with the flood--
In her right hand the lily, in her left
The letter--all her bright hair streaming down--
And all the coverlid was cloth of gold
Drawn to her waist, and she herself in white
All but her face, and that clear-featured face
Was lovely, for she did not seem as dead,
But fast asleep, and lay as though she smiled.

That day Sir Lancelot at the palace craved
Audience of Guinevere, to give at last,
The price of half a realm, his costly gift,
Hard-won and hardly won with bruise and blow,
With deaths of others, and almost his own,
The nine-years-fought-for diamonds: for he saw
One of her house, and sent him to the Queen
Bearing his wish, whereto the Queen agreed
With such and so unmoved a majesty
She might have seemed her statue, but that he,
Low-drooping till he wellnigh kissed her feet
For loyal awe, saw with a sidelong eye
The shadow of some piece of pointed lace,
In the Queen's shadow, vibrate on the walls,
And parted, laughing in his courtly heart.

All in an oriel on the summer side,
Vine-clad, of Arthur's palace toward the stream,
They met, and Lancelot kneeling uttered, 'Queen,
Lady, my liege, in whom I have my joy,
Take, what I had not won except for you,
These jewels, and make me happy, making them
An armlet for the roundest arm on earth,
Or necklace for a neck to which the swan's
Is tawnier than her cygnet's: these are words:
Your beauty is your beauty, and I sin
In speaking, yet O grant my worship of it
Words, as we grant grief tears. Such sin in words
Perchance, we both can pardon: but, my Queen,
I hear of rumours flying through your court.
Our bond, as not the bond of man and wife,
Should have in it an absoluter trust
To make up that defect: let rumours be:
When did not rumours fly? these, as I trust
That you trust me in your own nobleness,
I may not well believe that you believe.'

While thus he spoke, half turned away, the Queen
Brake from the vast oriel-embowering vine
Leaf after leaf, and tore, and cast them off,
Till all the place whereon she stood was green;
Then, when he ceased, in one cold passive hand
Received at once and laid aside the gems
There on a table near her, and replied:

'It may be, I am quicker of belief
Than you believe me, Lancelot of the Lake.
Our bond is not the bond of man and wife.
This good is in it, whatsoe'er of ill,
It can be broken easier. I for you
This many a year have done despite and wrong
To one whom ever in my heart of hearts
I did acknowledge nobler. What are these?
Diamonds for me! they had been thrice their worth
Being your gift, had you not lost your own.
To loyal hearts the value of all gifts

Must vary as the giver's. Not for me!
For her! for your new fancy. Only this
Grant me, I pray you: have your joys apart.
I doubt not that however changed, you keep
So much of what is graceful: and myself
Would shun to break those bounds of courtesy
In which as Arthur's Queen I move and rule:
So cannot speak my mind. An end to this!
A strange one! yet I take it with Amen.
So pray you, add my diamonds to her pearls;
Deck her with these; tell her, she shines me down:
An armlet for an arm to which the Queen's
Is haggard, or a necklace for a neck
O as much fairer--as a faith once fair
Was richer than these diamonds--hers not mine--
Nay, by the mother of our Lord himself,
Or hers or mine, mine now to work my will--
She shall not have them.' Saying which
she seized,
And, through the casement standing wide for heat,
Flung them, and down they flashed, and smote the
stream.
Then from the smitten surface flashed, as it were,
Diamonds to meet them, and they past away.
Then while Sir Lancelot leant, in half disdain
At love, life, all things, on the window ledge,
Close underneath his eyes, and right across
Where these had fallen, slowly past the barge.
Whereon the lily maid of Astolat
Lay smiling, like a star in blackest night.

But the wild Queen, who saw not, burst away
To weep and wail in secret; and the barge,
On to the palace-doorway sliding, paused.
There two stood armed, and kept the door; to whom,
All up the marble stair, tier over tier,
Were added mouths that gaped, and eyes that asked
'What is it?' but that oarsman's haggard face,
As hard and still as is the face that men
Shape to their fancy's eye from broken rocks

On some cliff-side, appalled them, and they said
'He is enchanted, cannot speak--and she,
Look how she sleeps--the Fairy Queen, so fair!
Yea, but how pale! what are they? flesh and blood?
Or come to take the King to Fairyland?
For some do hold our Arthur cannot die,
But that he passes into Fairyland.'

While thus they babbled of the King, the King
Came girt with knights: then turned the tongueless man
From the half-face to the full eye, and rose
And pointed to the damsel, and the doors.
So Arthur bad the meek Sir Percivale
And pure Sir Galahad to uplift the maid;
And reverently they bore her into hall.
Then came the fine Gawain and wondered at her,
And Lancelot later came and mused at her,
And last the Queen herself, and pitied her:
But Arthur spied the letter in her hand,
Stoopt, took, brake seal, and read it; this was all:

'Most noble lord, Sir Lancelot of the Lake,
I, sometime called the maid of Astolat,
Come, for you left me taking no farewell,
Hither, to take my last farewell of you.
I loved you, and my love had no return,
And therefore my true love has been my death.
And therefore to our Lady Guinevere,
And to all other ladies, I make moan:
Pray for my soul, and yield me burial.
Pray for my soul thou too, Sir Lancelot,
As thou art a knight peerless.'

Thus he read;
And ever in the reading, lords and dames
Wept, looking often from his face who read
To hers which lay so silent, and at times,
So touched were they, half-thinking that her lips,
Who had devised the letter, moved again.

Then freely spoke Sir Lancelot to them all:
'My lord liege Arthur, and all ye that hear,
Know that for this most gentle maiden's death
Right heavy am I; for good she was and true,
But loved me with a love beyond all love
In women, whomsoever I have known.
Yet to be loved makes not to love again;
Not at my years, however it hold in youth.
I swear by truth and knighthood that I gave
No cause, not willingly, for such a love:
To this I call my friends in testimony,
Her brethren, and her father, who himself
Besought me to be plain and blunt, and use,
To break her passion, some discourtesy
Against my nature: what I could, I did.
I left her and I bad her no farewell;
Though, had I dreamt the damsel would have died,
I might have put my wits to some rough use,
And helped her from herself.'

Then said the Queen
(Sea was her wrath, yet working after storm)
'Ye might at least have done her so much grace,
Fair lord, as would have helped her from her death.'
He raised his head, their eyes met and hers fell,
He adding,
'Queen, she would not be content
Save that I wedded her, which could not be.
Then might she follow me through the world, she asked;
It could not be. I told her that her love
Was but the flash of youth, would darken down
To rise hereafter in a stiller flame
Toward one more worthy of her--then would I,
More specially were he, she wedded, poor,
Estate them with large land and territory
In mine own realm beyond the narrow seas,
To keep them in all joyance: more than this
I could not; this she would not, and she died.'

He pausing, Arthur answered, 'O my knight,

It will be to thy worship, as my knight,
And mine, as head of all our Table Round,
To see that she be buried worshipfully.'

So toward that shrine which then in all the realm
Was richest, Arthur leading, slowly went
The marshalled Order of their Table Round,
And Lancelot sad beyond his wont, to see
The maiden buried, not as one unknown,
Nor meanly, but with gorgeous obsequies,
And mass, and rolling music, like a queen.
And when the knights had laid her comely head
Low in the dust of half-forgotten kings,
Then Arthur spake among them, 'Let her tomb
Be costly, and her image thereupon,
And let the shield of Lancelot at her feet
Be carven, and her lily in her hand.
And let the story of her dolorous voyage
For all true hearts be blazoned on her tomb
In letters gold and azure!' which was wrought
Thereafter; but when now the lords and dames
And people, from the high door streaming, brake
Disorderly, as homeward each, the Queen,
Who marked Sir Lancelot where he moved apart,
Drew near, and sighed in passing, 'Lancelot,
Forgive me; mine was jealousy in love.'
He answered with his eyes upon the ground,
'That is love's curse; pass on, my Queen, forgiven.'
But Arthur, who beheld his cloudy brows,
Approached him, and with full affection said,

'Lancelot, my Lancelot, thou in whom I have
Most joy and most affiance, for I know
What thou hast been in battle by my side,
And many a time have watched thee at the tilt
Strike down the lusty and long practised knight,
And let the younger and unskilled go by
To win his honour and to make his name,
And loved thy courtesies and thee, a man
Made to be loved; but now I would to God,

Seeing the homeless trouble in thine eyes,
Thou couldst have loved this maiden, shaped, it seems,
By God for thee alone, and from her face,
If one may judge the living by the dead,
Delicately pure and marvellously fair,
Who might have brought thee, now a lonely man
Wifeless and heirless, noble issue, sons
Born to the glory of thine name and fame,
My knight, the great Sir Lancelot of the Lake.'

Then answered Lancelot, 'Fair she was, my King,
Pure, as you ever wish your knights to be.
To doubt her fairness were to want an eye,
To doubt her pureness were to want a heart--
Yea, to be loved, if what is worthy love
Could bind him, but free love will not be bound.'

'Free love, so bound, were fre st,' said the King.
'Let love be free; free love is for the best:
And, after heaven, on our dull side of death,
What should be best, if not so pure a love
Clothed in so pure a loveliness? yet thee
She failed to bind, though being, as I think,
Unbound as yet, and gentle, as I know.'

And Lancelot answered nothing, but he went,
And at the inrunning of a little brook
Sat by the river in a cove, and watched
The high reed wave, and lifted up his eyes
And saw the barge that brought her moving down,
Far-off, a blot upon the stream, and said
Low in himself, 'Ah simple heart and sweet,
Ye loved me, damsel, surely with a love
Far tenderer than my Queen's. Pray for thy soul?
Ay, that will I. Farewell too--now at last--
Farewell, fair lily. "Jealousy in love?"
Not rather dead love's harsh heir, jealous pride?
Queen, if I grant the jealousy as of love,
May not your crescent fear for name and fame
Speak, as it waxes, of a love that wanes?

Why did the King dwell on my name to me?
Mine own name shames me, seeming a reproach,
Lancelot, whom the Lady of the Lake
Caught from his mother's arms--the wondrous one
Who passes through the vision of the night--
She chanted snatches of mysterious hymns
Heard on the winding waters, eve and morn
She kissed me saying, "Thou art fair, my child,
As a king's son," and often in her arms
She bare me, pacing on the dusky mere.
Would she had drowned me in it, where'er it be!
For what am I? what profits me my name
Of greatest knight? I fought for it, and have it:
Pleasure to have it, none; to lose it, pain;
Now grown a part of me: but what use in it?
To make men worse by making my sin known?
Or sin seem less, the sinner seeming great?
Alas for Arthur's greatest knight, a man
Not after Arthur's heart! I needs must break
These bonds that so defame me: not without
She wills it: would I, if she willed it? nay,
Who knows? but if I would not, then may God,
I pray him, send a sudden Angel down
To seize me by the hair and bear me far,
And fling me deep in that forgotten mere,
Among the tumbled fragments of the hills.'

So groaned Sir Lancelot in remorseful pain,
Not knowing he should die a holy man.